But No Candy

by GLORIA HOUSTON

illustrations by

LLOYD BLOOM

Philomel Books

New York

For Jennifer Margaret Houston,
my wonderful niece.—G.H.

To my sister, Betty, and Michael and Benjamin.—L.B.

Text copyright © 1992 by Gloria Houston. Illustrations copyright © 1992 by Lloyd Bloom. All rights reserved. This book, or parts thereof, may not be reproduced in any form without permission in writing from the publisher. Philomel Books, a division of The Putnam & Grosset Book Group, 200 Madison Avenue, New York, NY 10016. Published simultaneously in Canada. Printed in Hong Kong by South China Printing Co. (1988) Ltd. Book design by Nanette Stevenson. The text is set in Aldus. Library of Congress Cataloging-in-Publication Data. Houston, Gloria. But no candy / by Gloria Houston; illustrated by Lloyd Bloom. p. cm. Summary: While her Uncle Ted is off fighting in World War II, Lee watches the candy gradually disappear from the shelves of her family's store and realizes that her entire world has changed. ISBN 0-399-22142-5 [1. *World War, 1939-1945*—United States—Fiction. 2. Candy—Fiction. 3. Stores, Retail—Fiction. 4. Uncles—Fiction.] I. Bloom, Lloyd, ill. II. Title. PZ7.H8184Wh 1992 [E]—dc20 91-17883 CIP AC

13 5 7 9 10 8 6 4 2

First Impression

Lee and her family lived in an apartment above her daddy's big general store. The sign hanging over the double front doors read "Sunny Brook Store." Everyone up and down the River Road shopped there.

The afternoon was Lee's favorite part of the day, because if she was good, Lee was allowed to take a nickel from Mama's flowered dish in the kitchen cupboard and go to the big glass showcase to choose a treat.

Sometimes she chose peanut butter kits—a whole handful for a nickel. Sometimes she chose candy ice-cream cones. Once in a while, she chose orange gumdrops. But usually she chose a Hershey chocolate bar.

Then Lee would go to the shiny black cash register and Daddy would lift her up so she could press the button marked with a 5 and drop her nickel into the little box with all the other nickels.

If the weather was nice, before she ate her candy bar, Lee would climb to her secret place high in the hickory tree Daddy had planted in the sideyard. When she was safely wedged in where the branches of the tree formed a seat, Lee took the Hershey bar out of her pocket. First, she sniffed the chocolate through the brown and silver paper. Nothing else in the world ever smelled so good. Then she slowly took off the wrapper and smoothed it on her knees. Finally she unfolded the white paper and ate the little squares one at a time, letting the chocolate melt on her tongue. To Lee, the taste of that chocolate bar was the best thing in the world.

The days passed and soon it was time for Lee to ride the big yellow school bus to first grade. And each afternoon when she came home from school, the first thing she did was to take a nickel from the flowered dish to buy her candy bar.

Every night the neighbors would come over to sit around the big stove with the silver lace around the top that warmed the back of the store and listen to Daddy's big brown radio. Now that Lee was six years old she could stay up an hour later and listen, too.

"H. V. Kaltenborn and the news," said a deep booming voice coming from the radio. Lee put her hands over her ears because the sound reminded her of a bear growling.

"The war in Europe goes on," he said. "And in the Pacific, our ships are at sea." He talked about airplanes and bombs, and generals and Allies and Axis.

Lee listened quietly. She was not sure what the war was, but it did not sound good. The neighbors shook their heads, and everyone seemed very worried.

One day Uncle Ted came to the store wearing a brand-new green uniform and looking very handsome. In his pocket he had hidden two Hershey bars. He took them out and handed one to Lee and one to her brother, Tommy. He gave Mama, Tommy, and Lee each a hug and shook hands with Daddy. Then he got on the big gray and white bus that drove off down the road. Lee waved good-bye to Uncle Ted at the window.

"Where is Uncle Ted going?" asked Lee.

"He is going off to the war," said Daddy.

"I don't want him to leave," said Lee.

"He has to fight for his country. We are very proud of our soldier boy," said Mama with a big smile, but her voice wasn't smiling and there were tears in her eyes.

As the days passed, Lee saw fewer and fewer boxes of candy on the shelves of the big glass showcase. One day the shelves were bare, and Lee went to find out why.

"Why is the candy showcase empty, Daddy?" she asked.

"Because sugar is used to make candy for the soldiers like Uncle Ted," said Daddy. "That is part of the war effort."

"Why do the soldiers need candy?" said Lee.

"The soldiers are fighting hard in the war," said Daddy, "and candy is one of the foods they carry with them. We have to make sure they have the food they need to stay strong."

"I don't like the war," said Lee.

Daddy looked very sad. He said, "Honey, nobody likes war."

So the days passed. The salesman's little truck came. It carried pocket combs and writing tablets and laces for shoes. But no candy.

The bread truck came. It brought bread and rolls. But no candy.

The milktruck came. It brought milk and cream. But no candy.

The gasoline truck came. It brought gas and oil. But no candy.

So Lee knew the war must still be on. Daddy had said that when the war was over there would be candy again.

Soon it was time to go back to school. Lee was good at arithmetic. When she showed Daddy how well she could add and subtract, he gave her a very important job in the store. After school and on Saturdays she helped Daddy collect ration stamps from customers for gasoline. He pumped the swirling orange gasoline up to the glass top of the tall pump so it could rush through the black hose, and into the tanks of the cars. Carefully Lee counted the correct number of stamps. Daddy helped her collect the money and count the change back into the customers' hands.

When Mama wrote a letter to Uncle Ted, Lee took out her yellow pencil. She wrote a letter, too. The letter said,

Dear Uncle Ted,

I miss you. When are you coming home?

Love, Lee

P. S. When you come will you bring some candy, please? I would like a chocolate bar.

One cold winter afternoon Mama said, "The gypsy traders are here. Stay out of Daddy's way until their wagons are gone."

Lee took her brother upstairs, and Lee and Tommy stayed upstairs all that day. They looked out the center window over the "Sunny Brook Store" sign to see the brightly painted wagons camped in the grove of pine trees. Late that night Lee knelt in front of the window and rested her chin on the windowsill. She watched the campfires burning, and listened to the music of mandolins and accordions.

The next day a tall man with a mustache drooping down each side of his mouth walked across the road to the store. Tommy and Lee leaned far out the window to watch him go through the big front doors. The man carried a small wooden chest.

"Trade?" the man asked Daddy.

"What will you trade?" asked Daddy.

"Candy," said the man. "Candy for nails to mend our wagons."

"Valentine's Day is coming," said Daddy. "That's a fair trade." So the man left with a poke full of nails.

Daddy gave the little wooden chest to Mama.

"For Valentine's Day," Daddy said softly to Mama. She blushed.

Soon Mama came upstairs. She carried the little box up to her bedroom and set it on the dresser. Lee and Tommy peered around the door.

When Mama had gone, Lee pulled out the bottom drawer of the dresser just enough to stand on it. She opened the lid of the little chest.

"It's candy," she told Tommy.

That afternoon, when lunchtime was over, Lee climbed up on Daddy's lap. She gave him a hug and said, "Now we have candy. May I have some?"

But Daddy shook his head.

"That candy is a present for your mother," he said. "She will open it on Valentine's Day."

"When is that?" asked Lee.

"In a week," said Daddy.

Every day Lee and Tommy pulled out the drawers on Mama's big dresser. They climbed up and looked at the chest with the candy inside. It was covered all over with cellophane paper, but they could see the caramels and chocolate-covered cherries, and a mint or two in gold paper.

On Sunday afternoon, Lee and Tommy were drawing pictures. "Is it Valentine's Day yet?" asked Lee.

"No, not until Friday," said Mama. She looked out the window for a moment. Then she said, "But Valentine's Day means love, and I love you today. We won't wait for Valentine's Day."

Mama picked up the chest and carried it back to her bed. She tore the cellophane off the top of the chest and handed Lee and Tommy each a caramel. Then she carefully rewrapped the cellophane back over the little wooden chest.

"We'll have one piece a day as long as it lasts," she said.

So every day Mama gave them each a piece of candy. They ate it slowly, making it last a long while. And Lee never saw Mama eat a single piece of the candy herself.

Finally one day the chest was empty. Every once in a while, Lee would climb up to see if one piece might still be there, hidden in the corner of the chest. But now the chest and the big candy showcase in the store were empty.

"That must mean the war is *still* on," Lee told Tommy. "That's what Daddy said."

They sat on the little front porch of the store. Lee sighed and Tommy sighed, too. The war seemed to last an awfully long time.

Sometimes Lee sat on Daddy's lap when he read the newspaper. He helped her with the words so she could read with him. The top of Daddy's newspaper had *1943* on it.

When the numbers said *1944,* Lee could read more of the words.

And the war news still came on the radio. Lee stopped putting her hands over her ears and started listening.

Then one night, Daddy and Mama took Lee and Tommy to see the newsreels at the movie theater in town.

There Lee saw what a war looked like: airplanes dropping bombs, and soldiers marching with guns and running up beaches. Lee didn't like what she saw.

"Where is Uncle Ted?" she asked. "I don't see him anywhere."

"Sh-sh-h-h!" said Daddy.

On the way home from the show, Lee sat between Mama and Daddy in the front seat of the car. She leaned her head against Mama's arm.

"Will the war ever be over?" she asked.

"Will we ever have candy again?" asked Tommy.

Mama hugged Lee and kissed Tommy's curls.

"Yes, my darlings. Some day."

At school Lee's teacher announced that each grade would have a Scrap Metal Drive to help in the war effort. Lee wanted the fourth grade to win the contest.

Lee and Tommy found some old horseshoes and barbed wire in the meadow on the hill behind the store. Lee took them to school. She got a certificate with a gold border that said, "I am a good citizen. I helped in the war effort." It had Lee's name on it.

"You helped, too," she told Tommy.

So she took her yellow pencil and wrote Tommy's name on it, too.

At last Daddy's *Asheville Citizen* newspaper had *1945* printed at the top of the page, and before Lee realized it summer had arrived. One day just after school was out for vacation, the headline read: *V-E DAY! THE WAR IN EUROPE IS OVER!*

"Ted will be home soon from Italy!" said Mama. "His last letter said he would be home as soon as the European fighting was over!"

"Hooray! The was is over!" yelled Lee and Tommy, dancing around and around.

"Not quite," said Daddy. "The war is still being fought on the other side of the world."

So the family listened to the war news each night and hoped Uncle Ted would be home soon. But no word came.

Each day Lee's family and several of the store's customers waited for the big gray and white bus to make its stop. Some days people in the community stepped down from the bus. Other days the driver just waved as he passed. But no men wearing green uniforms ever got off.

Then one day in late summer, Lee was reading in her favorite hiding place high in the hickory tree in the sideyard. Suddenly the bells in the church on the hill began to ring. Cars rushed up and down the road in front of the store. The drivers honked their horns loudly. Everyone who stopped at the store laughed and shook hands and hugged one another, even the men. Lee watched from her perch in the tree. She climbed down to find Daddy.

"What is happening?" she asked.

"The war is over," Daddy said. "It is V-J Day! The war in the Pacific has been won!"

The whole family gathered on the porch under the sign that read "Sunny Brook Store." They waved at the drivers of the cars that whizzed past.

The big gray bus stopped in the road in front of the store.

The driver waved at the family. First, Mr. Biggerstaff stepped off wearing his white hat. Then Mr. Heaton stepped down, stuck his thumbs under his suspenders and marched across the road.

Just then a man in a dark green uniform stepped down. He carried a green bag. "Ted," shouted Mama as she dashed across the road.

"Uncle Ted," Lee shouted, following her with Daddy and Tommy close behind.

The whole family hugged him at the same time, and Mama wouldn't let go of him. "Ted, you're a sight for sore eyes," said Daddy. He just kept on shaking Uncle Ted's hand.

"What's for dinner?" said Ted. "I'm starved. I've been dreaming about some food from home. Is the sweet corn ripe yet?"

"The roasting ears have just come in. I'll go start dinner right away," said Mama, but she didn't leave.

"Oh, I forgot. I have something to deliver first," said Uncle Ted.

He unbuttoned the bag and took out something that was brown with silver letters.

A Hershey bar.

He handed one to Lee and one to Tommy.

"Sorry it took me so long to answer your letter, Lee."

"Thank you, Uncle Ted," said Lee. Tommy was already eating his candy bar. Uncle Ted smiled and Mama lead him into the house.

Lee could hardly wait to eat the chocolate bar somewhere all by herself, where she could savor every moment of it. She climbed back up into the hickory tree to her secret hiding place and wedged herself into the branches that formed a seat.

She wanted everything to be just like it used to be. First she smelled the chocolate bar. Then she unwrapped the brown and silver wrapper and smoothed it on her knees. Finally she opened the white paper and looked at all the little chocolate squares. She broke off one square and carefully placed it on her tongue.

Lee tried to remember how a chocolate bar tasted before the war, but she couldn't. Something felt different. Something had changed.

She could hear Uncle Ted's voice coming through the screen door of the kitchen. She wanted to talk to him, to be close to him, instead of sitting in her tree alone.

For a long while she stared at the candy squares. She had waited *so* long to taste it, but it just didn't seem as important as it used to be.

She folded the rest of the candy in the wrapper and tucked it into her pocket. She climbed down from the tree, and walked toward the kitchen door.

The hickory tree looked just the same. The big store looked the same. Even the blue sky was just the same.

But somehow at that moment Lee knew her world had changed. She had changed. She would never be the same again.

"Uncle Ted, I'm glad you're home," she said shyly as she opened the screen door.

"Lee, how you've grown!" said Uncle Ted. "You're a big girl now."

"Yeah," she said. She was almost as tall as his shoulder. Then she sat down beside him. "I guess I am."